THE STRANGE CASE OF WILLOUGHBY SPALDING

A Short Story

By Megan Wilcox

The Strange Case of Willoughby Spalding

Copyright © 2019 Megan Wilcox
All rights reserved.

No parts of this publication may be reproduced, stored in a retrieval system, or transmitted in any form or by any means, electronics, mechanical, photocopying, recording or otherwise, without the prior written permission of the copyright owner.

This book is sold subject to the condition that it shall not, by way of trade or otherwise, be lent, resold, hired out, or otherwise circulated without the publisher's prior consent in any form of binding or cover other than that in which it is published and without a similar condition including this condition being imposed on the subsequent purchaser. Under no circumstances may any part of this book be photocopied for resale.

This is a work of fiction. Any similarity between the characters and situations within its pages and places or persons, living or dead, is unintentional and purely coincidental.

ISBN-10: 1983940100

ISBN-13: 978-1983940101

Cover design: Bethany C. Willcock - Copyright © 2019

https://coverbookdesigns.weebly.com/

CONTENTS

Chapter 1 – pg. 4

Chapter 2 – pg. 11

Chapter 3 – pg. 24

Chapter 4 – pg. 39

Chapter 5 – pg. 46

Epilogue – pg. 52

About the Author – pg. 54

CHAPTER 1

"Here's the latest case file you asked for, Inspector Spalding."

The twenty-something police officer looked up from his place at his desk, and smiled at his secretary.

"Ah, thank you Elizabeth. Just set them there."

The young dark-haired woman nodded and set the files down. "Mr. Spalding—"

The man looked up again from the notes he was writing and shook his head. "Please, I've told you before; call me Will."

Elizabeth lowered her head and turned slightly red.

"S-sorry...Will. I—I was wondering; may I have the rest of the night off? A couple of my friends and I are planning on going to the pub."

Will grinned and reached for the cream envelope. "Oh yes. Go right ahead. I'll be leaving soon myself. Have fun."

The young woman's face lit up. "Thank you!"

The Strange Case of Willoughby Spalding

She spun around on her heels, and practically danced out of the Inspector's office.

Will shook his head, smiled, and pulled the papers from the file he had been given.

Inside was a missing persons file that was sent in from main police headquarters.

Studying the case notes, Will became interested in the seemingly impossible mystery of a child that had gone missing twenty years ago.

"Twenty years? It's about time for this boy's case to be taken into interest. Poor fellow..."

He read on, reviewing the strange case.

A young lad of five years old was sent to an orphanage after his parents allegedly died, and he was adopted soon after; but the orphanage burnt down a while later, destroying all records. Just five years ago, the mother of the boy was found to be alive and living on a remote island near Italy.

She and her husband had been shipwrecked on a journey to Morocco. Only she and another fellow survived.

The man and the mother, unable to reach civilization, married themselves a year after the wreck.
Upon being rescued, they were properly married.

Now the woman had her mind set on finding her seemingly long-lost son, and had come to the police, begging for help.

Will rubbed his clean-shaven chin, and slid the case notes back into the folder.

"Well now. I've got an interesting case on my hands

Megan Wilcox

for sure..."

He looked up at a painting hung on the wall. It was a serene landscape overlooking a field.

With a sigh, Will glanced down at the small stack of papers. "Now. I need to find this young William..."

He picked up and thumbed through the papers. "Ah yes. Let's see...Description: Plump, short, blond hair, brown eyes..."

He looked up at the ceiling in concentration. "So...Since it's twenty years later, the young fellow should be..."

He glanced back at the papers, and bit his lip. "Perhaps Roger will draw up an illustration of what he might look like now."

Nodding to himself, the detective picked up the description paper; taking it into the next room.

"Oh Roger?"

A middle-aged man looked up from his desk. "Yes Inspector?"

Will handed the paper over. "Do you think you can draw a bit of a picture from this?"

The man took it and looked it over. "Mmm yes. I think so. I'll have it ready for you in the morning."

Will grinned. "Thanks! I'll check in with you tomorrow then. I think I'll be leaving now. It's getting late."

Roger leaned back in his chair. "That is a good idea. I think I'll be leavin' meself in a short while."

Will nodded and placed his dark blue fedora on his head. "Goodnight then, Roger."

"Goodnight Inspector."

* * *

As Willoughby walked down the darkening streets, he mulled over the new case.

He came to the conclusion that it would be a good idea to interview the mother first thing in the morning; as was the normal procedure in such cases.

As he walked down the lamp-lit cobblestone road, Will realized that he was going in the wrong direction from his flat downtown.

"Oh bother..." He shook his head and turned about.

Going in the correct direction, he soon passed by the town pub.

"Hmm, perhaps I'll stop in for a drink."

Putting thoughts into action, Will found himself in the warm building that was a popular hangout for all of the townsfolk who wanted good drinks and conversation.

Wandering over to the counter, Will ordered some tea. The stout man behind the counter quickly got about filling his cup and slid the glass drinking vessel to the customer.

"There ya are, Will me lad."

Will nodded his thanks; taking a sip.

The bartender leaned across the counter slightly and watched the young man. "So! Any interesting cases today?"

Will glanced at the man and set his cup back down

on the counter. "Oh, nothing much more than the usual, Sam."

The bewhiskered man shrugged, and commenced drying a mug with a not-so-clean towel. "Ah, well. Can't blame a man for trying."

Will grinned and shook his head. "Sorry. I can't be revealing any police secrets to just anyone. Especially fellows who love to talk."

Sam straightened up. "I? Talk? Why, I'm as silent as the grave!"

Will chuckled and turned away from the counter to find a somewhat quieter place to finish his drink. He moved to the farthest corner of the pub and sat himself at a small table.

Looking out over the small crowd, Will did what was one of his favorite pastimes in crowded places; watching people, and how they acted, then guessing where they were from, and what their names might be.

Though that particular night, the game didn't last long on account that he knew just about every person there.

Will took another gulp of his warm beverage and noticed an approaching figure out of the corner of his eye. He looked up and saw his secretary. She didn't notice him, but continued talking with another young woman.

Will smiled, shook his head, and took another sip.

A minute later, Elizabeth noticed him, and walked over to his table. "Why, Mr.—Um, Will! I didn't know you were here."

Will slid out of his chair and stood up.

"I wasn't originally going to come here, but decided to at the last minute."

The young woman smiled and nodded to her companion. "Well, this is my older sister Claire. Claire, this is my commander, Will Spalding."

Will nodded and shook the sister's hand. "A pleasure to meet you miss."

Claire blushed, and giggled. "My goodness, I didn't realize that the police force had such good-looking fellows!"

Will couldn't help but be surprised at the forwardness of the young woman, when her sister was so meek and quiet. He pushed those thoughts aside and did what he thought was the mannerly thing to do. "Would you ladies like to join me? I've nearly finished my drink, but you're welcome to share my table."

Elizabeth glanced at her sister, who was nodding enthusiastically. Looking back at the Inspector, she slowly shook her head. "Thank you Will, but...Our friends over there will miss us if we don't go back and join them."

Will shrugged. "Suit yourself. Enjoy your evening, ladies."

As the two girls started away, Will called, "Don't be late to work tomorrow Liz. We've got quite a bit to go over."

Elizabeth glanced back at him and nodded.

Megan Wilcox

"Right. I won't be late. I'll see you in the morning."

CHAPTER 2

The next morning, Will arrived at the police station even earlier than usual, and paced in front of the entrance. About ten minutes later, Roger appeared; slightly out of breath.

"Oh, Will. I didn't realize you were going to be here so early. Sorry I'm late. I was up late workin' on those illustrations, and then had a bit of trouble with me bike this morning, so had to walk, but then, I was half way here when I realized that I had forgotten the papers..."

Will shrugged and walked in behind the man who unlocked the front doors.

"It's not a problem Roger. I had a bit of thinking to do while I waited."

Roger smiled and pulled a pile of papers out of his sack. "Well, anyway, here are your pictures. It's the best I could do with that blurry photograph provided."

Will gratefully accepted the artwork and looked at them studiously. "Mmm, these aren't too bad.

Splendid work, Rodge."

The man beamed and sat down at the front desk. "My pleasure."

Will took one more look at the drawings, then headed into his office where he pulled his papers out of the files and lined them up across his cork board, then stepped back to study the description and the illustrations that were drawn up from the written report.

As he stood in silence, carefully taking in every small detail, Elizabeth appeared in the doorway.

Other than looking somewhat tired, she was dressed up in her cream two-piece suit with a smart hat cocked to the side, and fresh red lipstick to finish off the outfit.

Will turned to greet her. "Ah there you are."

The young woman lowered her head. "Sorry I'm not early. I meant to, but I—Well. I suppose I stayed up too late last night."

Will nodded silently and glanced back over at his papers. "We've got a bit of interviewing to do today. I hope you're prepared to do a bit of driving."

Elizabeth stopped short and looked up at him in surprise. "*Interviewing* and *driving*?"

Will nodded, without looking at her. "Yes. I'm afraid that my normal driver is unable to come in this morning."

The young woman frowned and gave him a questioning look.

Will felt her gaze and glanced over his shoulder at

The Strange Case of Willoughby Spalding

her. "I have a medical condition called narcolepsy. I can fall asleep at the drop of a hat. I'm not capable of driving myself."

Elizabeth's eyes widened. "Oh. I didn't know..."

Will gathered the papers and started putting them back in the file. "I don't want to risk getting in a wreck. You don't mind driving, do you?"

The young secretary chewed her lip and shook her head. "No. I don't mind. It's no bother. I hope you feel better soon though, sir...Will."

Will smiled slightly at her and handed her the file. "Don't worry about it. Now. Can you find out where we can meet this woman? Her phone number is printed on the last page. Apparently, her address wasn't recorded."

The secretary nodded, and leaned over to pick up the phone, and started dialing the written number.

Will sat down in his chair and listened to the young woman.

"Hello, Mrs. Spinecroft? This is Elizabeth Archer down at police headquarters, we were wondering if you were available for an interview today? Yes...Where? Oh, the one next to the...yes. Yes...lunch? Very good. We'll see you then ma'am. Yes. Thank you. Goodbye."

She turned and smiled at her employer. "She suggested meeting at the small café at the end of town...Does that work for you?"

Will chuckled slightly. "Hmm, it seems it has to now."

Elizabeth blushed, and pursed her lips. "Sorry. I suppose I should have consulted with you on the location..."

Will drummed his fingers on the tabletop. "Well, we'll not worry about it this time."

The girl nodded slowly, took her seat, and set the papers aside. Her face was red from embarrassment until she caught the sparkle of mischief in Will's eye.

Will flashed a grin at her and looked back down at his paperwork.

Elizabeth felt her shoulders loosen, and she shook her head in amusement as she pulled her fountain pen out of the pen drawer.

❈ ❈ ❈

Will had been working diligently, reading over the different case notes, but his condition got the better of him, and he fell asleep within the hour.

A half an hour later, he woke with a start and realized what had happened.

He sat up and shook his head.

Elizabeth looked up from her paperwork and smiled at him. "Sleep well?"

Will felt his face turn red, and he sat up straighter in his chair. "What time is it?"

The secretary looked at a small gold-plated wrist watch strapped to her right wrist. "It's nearly ten o'clock sir."

Will groaned and rubbed his face. "Terribly

The Strange Case of Willoughby Spalding

sorry..."

The young woman smiled sweetly. "I understand sir, I mean, Will. I hope you're feeling better?"

Will nodded slowly and stood up. "Uh yes. I'm fine. Are you nearly finished? I think we should start for the café in order to get there before Mrs.—" He glanced at the paperwork lying on the desk. "—Spinecroft."

Elizabeth replaced her pen in its proper place, and also stood. "Good idea. Shall I bring the car around?"

Will glanced up at her and nodded as he stuffed the papers into a folder that he would be bringing along. "Yes. That would be fine. I'll meet you out front directly."

Elizabeth nodded silently and hurried out of the room.

Will smiled and shook his head at her disappearing figure. "I do hope that she doesn't forget the car in her hurry..."

He lifted his fedora from the hat hook and placed it on his head as he started toward the front door of the police station.

Roger looked up from the front desk. "Heading out? I saw miss Elizabeth scrambling by."

Will stopped and adjusted the shoulder strap of his leather bag. "Yes. I'm going to the café downtown to have an interview with the missing young man's mother. I'll be back within a few hours, I think. Anything I can grab for you while I'm there? A scone, or sandwich perhaps?"

Roger chuckled and rubbed his beard. "Well now. Nothing I can think of. I'll be fine. Me wife packed some leftovers from supper, so I doubt I'll be lacking for nourishment. Thank you though."

Will shrugged and nodded. "Suit yourself. I'll see you later. If there are any calls for me, just—"

"Write a note, and leave it on your desk. Aye. I know the drill."

Will grinned. "So you do. Right. Well, I'm off."

❊ ❊ ❊

A short while later, Will and Elizabeth were slowly making their way down the streets of the small town, toward the café where they would meet the missing boy's mother.

As they went, Will soon realized that Elizabeth was not only watching the road, but she also seemed to be looking at him from time to time.

"Miss Archer..." He started, agitatedly, "You're making me nervous."

Elizabeth's eyes widened, and she looked at him for a split second before turning her eyes back to the road.

"Why, what do you mean?"

Will rubbed his face in his hand and sighed. "You keep glancing at me, as if I was about to do something dreadfully exciting."

A bright red blush crept into the young woman's cheeks. "I-I'm sorry...I—I suppose I'm just..."

The Strange Case of Willoughby Spalding

She eased the car to a stop at the next stop sign, and folded her hands in her lap. "Does your...Narcolepsy...hurt?"

Will felt a smile try to grow on his lips, but quickly suppressed it; trying to act annoyed with his secretary.

"No, miss Archer. And I don't feel even the slightest bit tired."

Elizabeth gulped, and shifted the car back into gear, and eased them through the crossroad.

She said nothing the rest of the drive, which was only about two minutes more anyway.

Will studied her out of the corner of his eye as she pulled alongside the sidewalk in front of the café. "Elizabeth, I'm sorry for snapping at you."

She looked at him in surprise. "Oh no Will. I was being a pain. I deserved it."

Will smiled and reached out to pat her arm. "Well, I am sorry. But in answer to your question, I'm fine."

When she looked dubious, he nodded. "Truly."

They looked into each other's eyes for a half a moment, which caused Elizabeth's face to flare an even brighter shade of red.

She quickly lowered her eyes, and awkwardly fumbled to pull the car's key out of the ignition. "Well, I'm glad of that. Now, we'd better get in and find a table..."

Will, who also blushed slightly at the awkward moment, quickly exited the car, and they both went into the café without any more words exchanged.

A pretty young waitress met them at the door, and led them to an open table.

She excitedly handed them two menus. "What will it be today? Tea? Water?"

Will glanced at Elizabeth, who shrugged slightly, then he turned back to the short blonde girl. "Two teas, please."

The girl nodded and scurried off.

Will chuckled and shook his head. "Must be her first day."

Elizabeth nodded. "Could be. I don't recognize her."

Will cocked his head at her. "Oh, you've been here before?"

"Of course. Haven't you?"

Will slowly shook his head. "No. Well, yes. Once…I don't usually get out to eat very often. Just a stop at the pub on occasion."

Elizabeth's eyebrows raised up and down, "Ah. I see…"

The girl soon appeared with a teapot, and she promptly poured each of them a teacup full of a brown steamy liquid. "Are you going to be ordering something to eat?"

Will shook his head. "Not yet. We're meeting someone here."

At her fallen expression, Will quickly added, "But I'm sure we'll be ordering something to eat later. Just not yet."

The girl's face brightened once more, and she nodded. "Alright then! I'll be back to check on you two."

She smiled sweetly, and wandered away to another table, offering tea.

Will looked down at his cup, scooped two scoops of sugar in, then started stirring absentmindedly.

He then took a sip and checked his pocket watch. "She should be here anytime..."

He looked back at Elizabeth, who was holding her cup, staring into the contents.

"Something wrong with your tea, Liz?"

She looked up and shook her head sheepishly. "Nothing except the fact that it's tea."

Will felt his eyebrows raise. "Do you not like tea?"

She slowly shook her head and set the cup down. "Not particularly. I much prefer coffee, when it comes to it."

Will frowned. "Oh, I'm sorry. I should have asked before ordering."

She quickly waved him off. "Oh, it's fine. I like coffee, but not the stuff they serve here. It's so weak, one might mistake it for tea..."

Will grinned. "I didn't know you had a taste for coffee. Strong coffee at that, even. You surprise me, miss Archer."

Elizabeth raised an eyebrow and frowned. "Well now. I can't call you sir, but you call me miss?"

Will shrugged. "Good point. Elizabeth."

She smiled and nodded in satisfaction. "That's better..." She paused; her eyes moving to the entrance of the café.

Will followed her gaze, and saw a middle-aged couple coming in..

Nodding at his secretary, Will stood to meet them. "Mr. and Mrs. Spinecroft?"

The woman smiled and held her hand out. "Yes. You must be the Inspector?"

Will nodded, and shook both their hands, then led them to the table. "This is my secretary and driver, miss Archer."

Elizabeth smiled, and shook hands with the newcomers.

Once the foursome had seated themselves, Will wasted no time getting on with the case.

"So Mrs. Spinecroft, I have personally gone over the case, and hope to find your son in a timely manner. But I was hoping to ask a few questions about the young man."

The woman pulled a handkerchief from her purse and dabbed her eyes. "Yes, my poor little Willoughby."

Elizabeth looked at her employer. "Willoughby? Isn't that a funny coincidence!"

Will smiled at the bewildered look on the older woman's face. "My name is also Willoughby."

She nodded. "Oh! Such a lovely name..."

Will cleared his throat and continued. "Anyway, is there anything you can think of that you could tell me about him, that would possibly help in my investigation?"

The woman took a deep breath, and glanced at her

The Strange Case of Willoughby Spalding

husband, then she answered, "Well...Willy, as I called him for short, was a sweet lad. Though somewhat on the quiet side. He learned to read at a early age; Three. A "budding genius" the neighbors said..."

She sniffed and wiped her eyes with her handkerchief. "The poor fellow had no other relatives besides me and his father, rest his soul. So, when we were...shipwrecked, the authorities took him from our neighbors, where he was staying, and sent him to an orphanage."

Will nodded, scribbling down the story as she spoke. "Yes Ma'am. Have you spoken with those neighbors? Perhaps they..."

She shook her head; cutting him off. "Oh, I tried. But they've moved, and I haven't a clue as to where they are. Apparently, nobody in the entire town knows where they've gone. Probably America. Though I don't know what could possess someone to go there..."

Will frowned and rubbed his chin. "Right. So, is that all the information you can think of that could help in my investigation?"

Mrs. Spinecroft slowly shook her head, clearly at a loss of what else she could say.

Mr. Spinecroft, however, who had been silent up till then, leaned forward.

"One thing that might be useful; that orphanage that Willy was taken to, the one that burnt down, a colleague of mine named Michael Price knows someone who knows the former head of the orphanage. He works at the Quarry."

Will brightened slightly. "Brilliant! I think that sounds like a good lead. Thank you, sir."

The Spinecrofts looked at each other and smiled.

Mrs. Spinecroft leaned forward and placed her hand on Will's. "Thank you so much for helping us find my son. You're a good man."

Will, slightly flustered by the praise, pulled his hand back uncomfortably. "Oh, thank you ma'am. Really, it's not..."

Elizabeth smiled at the woman and patted her arm. "We'll be sure to let you know the minute we find out anything about your son, Mrs. Spinecroft."

The couple smiled their thanks and stood to leave.

Mr. Spinecroft shook Will's hand. "You have our number. See you soon, son."

Once the Spinecrofts had left, Will glanced down at the table, and back to Elizabeth who was still standing.

"Are you hungry? Because we can always get a bite to eat before heading out to the Quarry."

Elizabeth smiled slightly, and slid into her chair. "If you don't mind, I am quite hungry..."

Will nodded, and smiled. "Then we'll order some lunch. My treat."

The young woman opened her mouth to protest, but snapped it shut when Will shook his head.

"I insist. If you don't let me pay, we shan't eat at all."

Elizabeth smiled, and leaned back in her seat. "Fine then. You win."

Will nodded in satisfaction and waved the waitress over.

CHAPTER 3

An hour later, Will and Elizabeth pulled into the gravel drive of the town's Quarry.

A tall burly man met them at the entrance.

He tapped on the driver's window and motioned for her to roll it down. Upon her compliance, he leaned down and looked into the open window. "What's yur business?"

Elizabeth leaned back in apprehension, and stuttered out, "We...we need to speak to...to one of the workers here."

At the man's doubting look, Will pulled out his police identification card and held it out in front Elizabeth's stiff body for the man's inspection.

"Police investigation. We need to speak with a man said to work here."

The large man frowned, and rubbed his stubbly chin. "We don't need no trouble here, mister."

Will replaced his ID into his inner coat pocket. "No trouble sir. I just need to ask a man here a few questions. A Mister Price?"

The Strange Case of Willoughby Spalding

The man glanced at the closed Quarry gate, and nodded. "Very well. Just ask the man at the main building."

Will nodded his thanks as the man opened the gate. "Much obliged."

The guard merely grunted his response, and watched as the police car eased through.

Will noticed Elizabeth gripped the car wheel tighter than was usual.

"Liz, are you alright?"

She shrugged. "Perfectly, sir."

Will wasn't convinced, but let the subject drop when Elizabeth seemed unwilling to talk.

He made a mental note to ask her about what was wrong later. Something was up, and it wasn't good for a police inspector to not be able to trust his own driver.

* * *

They pulled up in front of the office building, and Will stepped out of the vehicle.

Leaning back in, he pulled out his briefcase. "You stay put. I'll be back shortly."

Elizabeth looked up and nodded as she turned the car's ignition into the off position. "Yes sir."

Will took a deep breath and marched into the office building.

He was met by a mousy man in a loose casual work outfit. The man wore large rimmed glasses and seemed to be a nervous sort.

"Y-yes?"

Will pulled out his identification and flashed it before the man's face. "Inspector Spalding here on a case. I'm looking for a man named Price. Michael Price."

The man nodded, but said nothing.

Will stared at him, waiting for directions to the man, but got no answer.

"Well?"

The man blinked. "Well what?"

Will sighed and drummed his fingers on the counter. "Can you tell me where I can find this man?"

The small man shrugged. "You've already found him."

Will rubbed his chin. "You're Michael?"

"Of course."

Will blew out an exasperated breath. "Well then. I need to ask you a few questions."

Mr. Price nodded and fiddled with a nearby pencil. "Fire away."

Will rubbed his hands together. "You know a man who works here, name of Spinecroft?"

"Yes."

"Well, I was speaking to the Spinecrofts earlier—"

The man gasped slightly and leaned forward in his chair. "They aren't in any trouble, are they?"

Will shook his head. "Ah, no. Not at all. You might know that they're in search of the madam's missing son?"

The Strange Case of Willoughby Spalding

Michael nodded and seemed to relax. "Yes."

"Anyway, they mentioned that you know someone who is acquainted with the owner of the orphanage that used to be in operation some years ago. Could you give me the name of that individual?"

The man shrugged. "Of course. I know the owner of the orphanage myself. But I doubt she'll be of much help, sir..."

Will held his hand up. "That will be for me to decide. Now. Could you give me her name and address?"

Mister Price nodded. "Oh yes...The name is Miriam O'Toole. She currently lives at her daughter's home on 5th street. You know where that is? She lives in the last house on the right side of the road. You can't miss it."

Will frowned as he scribbled out the instructions.

The last name seemed vaguely familiar.

"Right. Thank you for your help."

The small man stood and held his hand out tentatively. "Anything to help find the young man."

Will shook his hand. "Sorry for disrupting your day. I'll take my leave."

The man smiled faintly. "Not at all. You livened up this drab place. You can't imagine how lonely it can get in here when a man's working partner is home sick."

Will nodded, unsure of how to answer. "Yes...Well I hope your friend gets better soon."

Price brightened. "Thank you. I'm sure he'll be back soon. Thank you, Inspector."

* * *

Will then exited the building, and found the car right where he had left it, but there was an extra body.

A handsome young man was leaning against the car's hood, chatting away with a very uncomfortable looking Elizabeth, who was also standing outside of the vehicle.

Will walked over and set his case inside the passenger door.

The young man stopped his chatting and turned to look at Will.

Will frowned at him, and leaned against the roof of the car. "What's your business here?"

The ruddy young man straightened up and hung his thumbs in his belt loops. "I was about to ask you the same question."

Elizabeth glanced from one to the other, and spoke up in Will's defense. "This is my boss. Inspector Spalding."

The young man ran his eyes up and down, sizing Will up. "He doesn't look like an inspector to me."

Will narrowed his eyes at the man and put his hand on the door. "Well, that is your narrow-minded opinion, sir. Come Elizabeth. We need to get to the eastern side of town before supper."

Elizabeth nodded, and was about to get into the driver's seat, but the young man reached out a hand

The Strange Case of Willoughby Spalding

to stop her. "Hold on. You still haven't told me whether I can see you later."

Elizabeth frowned, and pulled her arm away. "I don't think that would be possible. Good day, sir."

The man was apparently unable to take "no" for an answer.

He stepped in her way to prevent her entering the vehicle. "Come now. Don't be that way..."

Will had had enough by that point, and walked around the side of the car. "Leave the young lady be. And step away from the car, now."

The young man sneered. "Who's going to make me?"

Will rolled his eyes and pulled back the corner of his coat to reveal a gun belt. "I am an officer of the law. I won't hesitate to bring you in for misconduct."

The young man's eyes widened slightly, and he stepped back away from the door.

Elizabeth quickly ducked in and closed her door before he could stop her again.

Will let his coat fall back to its place and pointed to the young man. "You'd better get back to your work before I report you to your manager."

The young man narrowed his eyes and glared at Will, but said nothing and backed away from the vehicle.

Will nodded to himself in satisfaction and went back around the car to get inside.

Elizabeth wasted no time in shifting the vehicle into gear and pulling out of the parking lot of the

Quarry.

Will looked at his secretary in concern. "Are you alright?"

She nodded her head quickly. "Yes."

Will frowned and glanced in the side view mirror as they drove through the gate.

"What's wrong?"

Elizabeth sighed slightly and glanced at him. "It's —"

He cut her off. "And don't tell me it's nothing. There's obviously something bothering you."

A frown formed as she slowly nodded. "Yes sir…"

Will waited for an explanation.

She bit her lip, and then explained herself. "It's just…My sister is in trouble. She's been kicked out of her flat for not paying bills, and has nowhere to go. I've invited her to stay at my flat, but I'm afraid she'll just get into more trouble."

Will frowned. "Anything illegal?"

She quickly shook her head. "Oh no."

Will nodded. "But…That doesn't tell me why you've been acting so strangely since we arrived at the Quarry."

She wrinkled her nose slightly. "I…I don't know. I suppose…"

She glanced at her handsome employer, and blushed. "It's silly, I know, but—"

Will cocked his head in curiosity. "What?"

"I'm afraid I've got an irrational fear of strangers… Particularly men."

The Strange Case of Willoughby Spalding

He raised his eyebrow. "You do?"

Elizabeth took a deep breath and nodded.

Will scratched his head. "But, you seemed perfectly fine around the Spinecrofts."

She shrugged. "Yes. But that's because I practically knew them. I don't have a reason to be uncomfortable around strangers, but I am."

Will shook his head in amazement. "I never noticed before."

"That's because I've never been out of the office with you before..."

"But..." Will countered, "You didn't seem at all apprehensive when you first met me."

She chuckled slightly. "Oh, I was. But I needed the job, and I knew who you were. Just not...personally."

"I see."

They fell silent.

Will was frowning to himself; mulling their conversation over in his head.

Elizabeth too, was thinking. She felt exposed after telling her employer her darkest secret.

She glanced at him as she carefully steered the car down the road, and then looked back to the road.

The young secretary felt her face turning red as she thought more about the conversation just held.

Will's own mind however, had wandered back to the case, and he didn't notice.

But when he glanced around the cab of the car, he realized the look on his secretary's face was anything but easy. "Liz?"

She jumped and looked at him. "What?"

Will reached out and tentatively touched her arm. "I'm sorry if I pried. It's really not any of my business."

Elizabeth pulled the car to a stop at a stop sign and smiled at him. "It... It's alright Will. I suppose one should know things about his secretary. Especially since you're an inspector, you would have found out about it sooner than later."

Will chuckled. "That still doesn't give me the right to pry."

Elizabeth's smile returned, "Please, don't fret about it Will. I..." She pressed the accelerator and eased the vehicle onto the cross road toward 5th street. "I actually feel better now that I've told you."

Will rubbed his neck but said nothing.

Elizabeth glanced in her rearview mirror, "So! Now you and I both have a secret we know about each other."

At Will's questioning look, she laughed slightly. "You're always sleepy, I'm scared."

Will chuckled. "Ah..." He narrowed his eyes at her and smiled. "I suppose that works. Yes..."

He pointed ahead. "Here. This is the place."

Elizabeth pulled the shift-stick into first gear and eased her way against the sidewalk. "So why are we here again?"

Will pulled his briefcase into his lap and reached for the door handle. "The lady who previously ran the orphanage lives here with her daughter."

The Strange Case of Willoughby Spalding

Elizabeth nodded, and put the vehicle into park. "Should I wait here?"

Will shrugged. "You don't have to. You're welcome to come..."

He stepped out of the car and took a deep breath. "They may not even be home, so you can wait until I check."

She nodded and watched him walk up to the large green door, and rap on it briskly.

He waited, and finally the door was opened by a woman in her mid-thirties.

She frowned and looked him over. "Yes? What do you want?"

Will removed his hat and stuffed it into his arm. "Hello, is this the O'Toole residence?"

The woman shifted on her feet and shrugged. "Maybe it is. What's your business?"

Will inwardly groaned at the inhospitable welcomings he had gotten all that morning, but ignored the annoyance and pulled out his badge once more. "My name is Inspector Will Spalding. I was wondering if I could have a word with Miriam O'Toole?"

There was a shuffling noise from behind the door, and it opened fully; revealing a small white-haired woman. She pushed who Will assumed was her daughter out of the way, and stood in the doorway; hands clasped together.

"Oh! A visitor? Do come in young man!"

Will glanced over his shoulder at his secretary, who shook her head in sign that she preferred to stay in the car.

Will nodded and stepped into the house; following the woman into a small living room.

The daughter sat next to her mother and watched Will suspiciously, which caused his face to involuntarily turn red.

He tried to ignore her however, and turned his attention to the smiling old woman.

She leaned forward in her seat. "So, what brings you here to visit me today, Willoughby?"

Will straightened up in surprise. "How did you know my name?"

The woman's face clouded slightly. "Why, how could I forget? You were one of the best lads in the orphanage."

Will shook his head and ran his hand through his hair. "I-I think you're mistaken ma'am. I..."

The woman's face went blank suddenly, and she looked at her daughter. "Dear, would you make some tea for our guest?"

The woman nodded sullenly, and disappeared out of the room.

Will didn't take his eyes off the older woman. His mind was whirling. He had been an orphan at one point in time. But his adoptive parents had gotten him from a different orphanage, in a town far away from the one this woman had run.

He rubbed his hands together and cleared his throat. "Mrs. O'Toole..."

The woman looked at him and frowned. "I'm

The Strange Case of Willoughby Spalding

sorry, what's your name again, young man?"

Will blinked in confusion, but told her his name again.

She merely nodded and smiled. "So, what brings you here, young sir?"

Will took a deep breath, and slowly explained to her the situation.

All acknowledgement of the earlier conversation seemed to be gone from the woman's memory.

She adjusted her skirt. "Well yes. I did work at, even owned the orphanage downtown. I loved that place..."

A faraway look came into her eyes, and she sighed slightly. "But then one day...I suppose it was that one boy. He really didn't like it there. He had had a hard life. One day, he just..."

She sniffed slightly. "At least everyone made it out safely. Nobody was lost. Just all the information about everything."

Will nodded and licked his lips in concentration. "I'm sorry. Mrs. O'Toole, do you remember anything about a young boy named Willoughby?"

The woman chewed her thin lip and rubbed her temples. "Oh...Yes. He was a sweet boy. Very kind. Yes...He was always helpful. A quiet boy. Very bright. Oh..."

She frowned, and her mind seemed to go blank. "Oh...? What did you say?"

Will huffed. "Do you know who adopted the young lad named Willoughby? His biological mother is searching for him."

The woman reached for the cup of tea her daughter had just brought in. "He was adopted three days before the fire. A family called Sirkis, or Crispin, I think."

She sighed. "Will promised to write, and keep in touch, but I never heard from him again—" Her face brightened. "–Until now."

Will slowly shook his head. "I'm not that Willoughby, Mrs. O'Toole."

The woman smiled slightly. "If you say so, dear."

Will glanced at the daughter, who still watched with narrowed eyes, then cleared his throat uncomfortably.

"Well, thank you for the information ma'am. I should probably be going."

Mrs. O'Toole smiled, and stood up. "Thank you for visiting, Willoughby. Do come back again."

Will smiled at the old woman and reached for the door handle. "I am busy, but I will try to visit you again sometime. Good day, ladies."

He placed the fedora on his head and exited the building.

Elizabeth spotted him right away and turned the awaiting car on.

The young detective plopped into the passenger seat and let out an exasperated sigh.

Elizabeth looked at him questioningly. "What's wrong? Wasn't she any help?"

Will frowned at his secretary and shook his head.

The Strange Case of Willoughby Spalding

"Not particularly. The poor woman must have a bad memory."

He rubbed his forehead. "And she kept thinking that *I* was the young man that was missing."

Elizabeth frowned, and pulled onto the roadway. "I'm sorry...Did you not find out anything?"

Will shrugged. "I'm not sure. I've gotten two names; Sirkis and Crispin. I'll have to look them up once we get back to the office."

Elizabeth glanced at the small golden watch around her wrist and nodded.

Will noticed her watch, and "hmm-ed".

"Oh...It's later than I thought. Would you...Would you like to stop for supper somewhere before returning to the office?"

Elizabeth shook her head quickly. "Oh. No thank you...My sister is home. She'll be waiting for me—" She glanced at him. "But thank you for the offer."

Will nodded silently, but kept staring ahead as they slowly moved along the narrow roads of the small British township.

The sun slowly set along the western horizon; shadows growing as each moment passed.

The inspector and his secretary rode in silence; Will's mind was occupied with the increasingly baffling case, and Elizabeth focused on the sudden change in the air between them.

She couldn't quite place it, but there seemed to be a certain tension in the air when Will and she were together. A tension that caused her heart to flutter ever so slightly.

Glancing at the young man seated beside her, she smiled to herself.

She and he would figure this case out soon. She was sure of it.

CHAPTER 4

That evening, as Will sat on his bedside, he pondered the strange case that had been placed before him.

The earlier conversation with Miriam O'Toole had him particularly confused.

He couldn't understand why she had confused him not once, but twice with the missing man, who also happened to have the same first name.

A sudden thought crossed his mind, but he quickly dismissed it.

"It's preposterous...The poor woman must not only have a bad memory, but be half blind. Besides... Boys never look the same as they do full grown."

With that thought, he turned under his soft bed covers, and soon fell into a fitful sleep.

A strange dream haunted Will as he tossed and turned that night.

He saw a young boy; himself, grasping a young woman's hand. He was crying while being led away by an unknown person.

Megan Wilcox

The woman knelt down and kissed him on the cheek; wiping away his tears.

"Don't cry, Willy. Papa and I will be back soon. You'll like staying at the neighbors'. They're very nice."
She hugged him and patted his soft blonde head.

"I love you..."

The whispered sentiment echoed throughout Will's head, and he awoke with a start.

"Mum!"

His blurry eyes swept the dark bedroom as he tried to regain his bearings.

He then realized that it had been a dream. He ran his sweaty hand over his light brown hair and took a deep breath. "Get a hold of yourself old boy. It was only a dream..."

He shook his head and laid back into his pillow.

❊ ❊ ❊

Sleep soon claimed him once again, and another dream passed through his unconscious mind. This time, he saw a young teenage boy sitting on the swings in a school playground.

Children were gathered around him, watching and listening as he told them a story.

"And that's how the chief inspector captured the entire gang. It was a brilliantly thought out plan."

The children all cheered at the end of the story.

One small girl stepped closer. "Is that why you want to be a inthpecter when you dwow up, Will?"

The Strange Case of Willoughby Spalding

The boy sat up proudly. "Naturally. I'm going to follow in my father's footsteps, until I'm a great Inspector like he was."

Another child piped up, "You'll be a thplendid offither, Will!"

The lad grinned and shrugged. "I'll try..."

He was interrupted by a sharp jab on his shoulder.

Will turned and came face to face with his enemy; a boy much too tall and muscular for his young age.

The bully sneered. "Hey look, it's Inspector Spalding."

Will got off the swing, and turned to face the boy, who had a few of his friends surrounding him. "What do you want, Alex?"

The tall boy scoffed. "Like the police would ever let an orphan into their ranks."

Will's face darkened, and he gripped the swing chains tightly. "I'm not an orphan!"

Alex rolled his eyes. "'Course you are. But of course, you wouldn't remember. You got a head injury right after the Spaldings adopted you. So you can't remember a thing."

Tears welled up in Will's eyes. "T-that's not true!"

The group of bullies all laughed and walked away.

Will leaned against the swing and gulped back the tears that threatened to spill, but they came anyway...

* * *

Will awakened with a gasp. He took a deep breath and shook his head. Peering at the clock on his bed-

Megan Wilcox

side table, he saw that it was four in the morning.

Deciding that it would be impossible to get to sleep again, he sat up and swung his legs over the side of the bed.

He frowned as he thought about his latest dream.

"E gad!"

A sudden rush of memory swept over him.

Ever since he could remember, he had lived with the Spaldings.

But when he confronted them about it, after that conversation with Alex; which he vividly remembered now, he found out that he had only lived with them since he was seven.

And he also found out that he did in fact have an accident which caused him to have what the doctors said to be just amnesia, but it had lasted ever since; no memories from before the age of seven surfacing.

Until now.

With that thought in his mind, Will jumped out of bed and rushed over to the telephone in the sitting room of his flat.

Picking up the receiver, Will dialed out the number of his beloved adopted parents.

He waited impatiently for the other end to be picked up.

Finally, a man's groggy voice answered. "H-hello?"

Will gripped the phone with both hands, and gasped out, "Father, it's me; Will. I need to speak with you. It's very important. Can you meet me somewhere?"

The Strange Case of Willoughby Spalding

The line was silent, then the man sighed. "Willoughby, do you realize what time it is?"

Will ignored his question. "Father, it is imperative that we meet."

The man on the other line huffed. "Ah...Very well. We obviously cannot meet in a café or anything. It's too early..."

Will rubbed his chin. "Mmm, that could be a problem...Father, do you mind meeting me in the park? It's nearer both you and I in locality."

There was silence, then the man replied, "I'll get ready."

Will nodded at the receiver; relief starting to calm his nervous mind. "Splendid. I'll see you in about forty-five minutes."

He then hung up and rubbed his hands together in anticipation. "Right now, I'd best get ready. I've got to get some answers."

※ ※ ※

An hour later, Will was seated on a bench beside his adoptive father.

The older man looked at the inspector questioningly when he said nothing for the first few minutes. "What is it, Willoughby?"

Will chewed his lip; hesitant to ask, but then took a deep breath and asked the question that was on his mind. "Father...I'm adopted."

Mr. Spalding frowned, and nodded silently.

Will cleared his throat and continued. "But I can't remember ever being anywhere but with you. Why is that?"

His father shook his head. "The doctors called it amnesia. You took quite a bad spill just a few weeks after we adopted you, knocked unconscious. When you awoke two days later, you couldn't remember a thing."

Will bit his lip and nodded. "Oh. I suppose that explains a bit...But father, was I...adopted by any other family, before coming to live with you and Mother?"

The man looked ahead of them at the slowly rising sun on the eastern horizon and took a deep breath.

"Why do you ask?"

Will sighed and leaned forward. "It's a long story actually. But I really need to know."

Mr. Spalding leaned back and licked his lips in thought. "The family that adopted you were unable to keep you. Their son, a few years older than you, caused so much trouble because of the new addition, they had to give you up. We adopted you a few days later."

Will frowned; the similarities between his and the missing boy's lives were becoming even more strange. He shook his head and bit his lip.

"Father, do you happen to know...do you know which orphanage it was that the other family adopted me from?"

His adoptive father raised an eyebrow in confu-

The Strange Case of Willoughby Spalding

sion, and slowly shook his head. "I'm afraid I don't. And you won't be finding it either. It burned down right after you left. It was all over the newspapers that week."

Will caught his breath and leaned forward to put his head in his shaking hands.

Mr. Spalding, even more baffled by his son's behavior, put his hand on the young man's back. "Why, whatever is the matter Willoughby? Are you alright?"

Will lifted his face and smiled slightly.

"Father, I think I've just solved my case."

CHAPTER 5

Later that morning, Will was waiting impatiently at his desk for his secretary to appear.

He was nearly beside himself with the newly found information about his case.

Once she arrived, they would be going to meet with Mr. and Mrs. Spinecroft to tell them what he had discovered.

A few minutes later, Elizabeth burst through the door; slightly out of breath.

Will cleared his throat in mock annoyance and twiddled a pencil around. "I hope you're not going to make a habit of coming to work late. It's really starting to get a bit on the annoying side."

Elizabeth lowered her head in shame and set her handbag on her desk. "I'm terribly sorry Will, I—"

She looked up again at her employer and finished lamely, "I'm sorry."

Will shook his head and tossed his pencil aside. "I'll forget about it this one last time. But don't let it happen again."

The Strange Case of Willoughby Spalding

He then broke into a smile, and he relaxed in his chair.

Elizabeth noticed his sudden change and cocked her head. "What is it?"

Will shook his head, and grinned. "I've solved the case Liz. I did it."

She frowned. "What? Really?"

Will stood up and nodded excitedly. "Yes."

The young woman's face lit up. "How? Where is he?"

He felt himself blush slightly. "He's right here."

Liz looked around the room in confusion. "I don't understand..."

Will reached for his briefcase. "That's because—I'm who I've been looking for."

Elizabeth's eyebrows shot up in shock. "You—you're not joking..."

Will shook his head; his face turning serious.

"I promise you, this is no joke. I've done all the research I can, and the missing man, and myself, are one and the same."

His secretary clasped her hands together. "Will! That's fantastic!" She impulsively threw her arms around his neck and hugged him tightly.

Will stiffened at the unexpected outburst, but allowed her to finish the hug.

When she stepped away, Liz gasped in realization at what she had done; her brown eyes widening. "Oh...sorry, I didn't mean to—"

Will felt his own face reddening. "W-we should be

going."

She lowered her head and followed him out of the office. "Where are we going?"

Will glanced over his shoulder at her. "We are going to meet the Spinecrofts. Please fetch the car."

Liz nodded silently and hurried out the door.

Will couldn't keep back his smile as he stopped by Roger's desk.

The older man looked up at him and smiled brightly.

"Congratulations on solving your latest case, Inspector. I knew you could do it."

Will shrugged, unable to repress his excited smile. "Thank you, Rodge."

He glanced out the front window, and spotted his secretary pulling the car up against the curb.

"Ah. I'd better go now. I've got some folks to meet."

Roger nodded. "Right you are. I'll see you in a bit then, Will."

Will nodded and started for the door, but paused for a second, and called back to his friend, "Oh, and you might want to work on your drawing skills Roger..."

He held up the rough illustration of the "missing person" and grinned mischievously. "This doesn't look a *bit* like me."

❋ ❋ ❋

The Strange Case of Willoughby Spalding

Later, at the café, Will waited excitedly for the Spinecrofts to arrive.

He sipped his tea nervously and kept looking out the window in expectation.

Elizabeth sat beside him; herself feeling the growing excitement of the solved case.

She reached out and put her small hand on Will's larger one.

He jumped at the unexpected touch and looked at her.

She smiled shyly and shrugged slightly. "Will, don't fret. They'll be here soon."

Will loosened his tight shoulders and sighed. "Ah, you're right..."

He reached his other hand over and patted hers. "You're a good friend, Liz."

He couldn't help but noticed that her smile faded ever so slightly at his comment, so he leaned forward slightly and whispered in her ear. "But I hope to change that."

When Will leaned back, he saw her face flush bright red, and her eyes shone.

"You mean...?"

He fingered his teacup and nodded slowly. "I mean it. Maybe not until next year, but I really do want—"

He stopped short when he caught sight of a middle-aged couple coming into the café, but shook his head when he realized that they weren't the expected visitors; just a couple coming in for a late morning brunch.

Will turned back to his still blushing secretary. "You don't mind if I call on you next week?"

She smiled brightly and shook her head. "Not at all.

I—I would like that."

Will returned her smile, and they sat there in silence for a few minutes.

Finally, the awaited couple arrived.

Mrs. Spinecroft was almost panting as she slid into a chair. "What's the news, Inspector?"

Will cleared his throat and folded his hands on the table. "I'm happy to tell you that after making short work of diligent searching and, well...you might say, some eye-opening events, I have come to the end of my search."

The older woman clasped her hands together. "Did you really? Where is my Willoughby now?"

Will cleared his throat and leaned back in his chair. "It's a bit strange..."

Her face clouded. "He's not—"

Will quickly shook his head. "Oh dear, no! He's actually...I'm...*I'm* your son."

Mrs. Spinecroft stared at him with a blank face.

"W—what? I don't think I follow..."

Will leaned forward. "It's true Ma'am. I am Willoughby. Everything I've come across in my investigation points to that fact."

A confused frown crossed the woman's face, and she took a shaky breath. "Will? You're...you're my boy?"

The Strange Case of Willoughby Spalding

Her eyes started to water, and she reached out to touch Will's cheek. "My Willoughby?" She caught her breath. "How is that possible?"

Will reached up his own hand and held the shaking woman's. "I didn't remember myself until last night. It seems I got a case of amnesia right after the Spaldings adopted me, so I don't really remember much about anything before I was seven."

Mr. Spinecroft, who had been quiet the entire conversation, shook his head. "That's a shame! I'm so sorry, my boy."

As Elizabeth watched the conversation, her eyes started to water, so she gripped her teacup, and sipped it slowly in attempt to distract herself.

Will cleared his throat again, and shrugged at his mother. "Well! This has been quite the interesting case. I started this case with one family, and now I have two."

Mrs. Spinecroft laughed softly, then leaned out of her chair, wrapped her arms around Will's neck, and started to sob quietly.

"Oh, my boy...my sweet, sweet boy! How I've longed for this day!"

Will closed his eyes happily and surrendered himself to the warm embrace of his long-lost mother.

EPILOGUE

Willoughby Spalding spent many of the following days catching up with his mother; learning about her, his father, and all the things that his young self and his biological family had done before being split up by tragedy.

The Spaldings and Spinecrofts became very good friends, and the fathers went fishing every Sunday afternoon after church, while the mothers spent their afternoons together as well.

Will also came to know his half-brother John; a friendly young lad thrilled at the prospect of having an older brother. The brothers spent many happy hours together; laughing, joking, and working together on cases, once John joined the police force as a constable.

Sundays were always a joyful time for Will; being able to spend time with his beloved families, but Saturdays were his particular favorite, as he spent each and every one of them with his fiancée, who happened to not only be his secretary, but his best friend;

Miss Elizabeth Archer.

ABOUT THE AUTHOR

Megan Wilcox is a Christian young woman who loves writing, painting, dancing, and playing her numerous instruments which include the piano, penny whistle, guitar, accordion, and violin. She lives on her family's farm in the Pacific Northwest, and enjoys volunteering at her local National Historic Site.

Made in the USA
Middletown, DE
05 May 2024